For Margaret Anastas,
who makes rosy-red dreams come true

Book and Florabelle character © 2015 by Catbird Productions, LLC

Text by Sasha Quinton
Illustrations by Brigette Barrager
Photography by Michel Tcherevkoff
Produced by Catbird Productions, LLC

ISBN 978-0-06-229182-0
Typography by Jeanne L. Hogle
15 16 17 18 19 PC 10 9 8 7 6 5 4 3 2 1
❖
First Edition

FLORABELLE

Written by Sasha Quinton

Illustrated by Brigette Barrager

with photographs by Michel Tcherevkoff

HARPER

An Imprint of HarperCollinsPublishers

Meet Florabelle.

She's a little girl with big rosy-red dreams.

"Keep your head out of the clouds!" her mother always tells her.

But Florabelle was much too busy dreaming to listen. "I bet it's beautiful up there. . . ."

That morning, Florabelle was too busy twirling
and swirling to join her family for breakfast. "I bet cereal
tastes better . . . when you're a ballerina!"

While getting dressed, her sister warned, "You'll be late again!"

But Florabelle didn't hear a word. "I bet school's more fun . . . when you're a fairy princess!"

At the bus stop, the driver honked
beep beep beeeep. But Her Highness
Florabelle didn't move a royal inch.
"I bet no one minds waiting for you . . .
when you're a queen!"

Florabelle's family was losing patience.
"Come back down to earth!" they begged.
Sometimes they were very, very serious.
(Too serious for Florabelle, anyway!)

At dinner, Florabelle Jean, Rodeo Queen, rode through the kitchen.
"That's it, Florabelle! You're in a time-out!" said her father.
"And we're not going to the beach tomorrow if you don't start
listening," her mother added.

Florabelle had always dreamed of going to the beach!
She couldn't take any chances!

Tomorrow she'd be serious. Very, very S-E-R-I-O-U-S. Just like her family.

The next morning, Florabelle was focused.
Her teeth were sparkling, her dog was fed, and her
bed had perfectly tucked corners.

She was even the first one in the car!
Everyone was happy. "Buckle up!" her father said.

But when they got to the beach, Florabelle was met
with an unhappy surprise.
   The sea was nothing like she'd imagined.
   It looked very deep . . .
      . . . and very dark
      . . . and very, *very undreamy*!

"Join us, Florabelle!"
"The water's warm!"
"One, two, three, jump!"
"No way; not me!" Florabelle replied.
"I'm staying put."

Florabelle refused to watch as her family dipped and dove, and Marigold happily doggy-paddled beside them.

Instead, back on land, Florabelle dug herself in deeper and doodled in the sand. "Who wants to swim in a big scary ocean, anyway?"

Suddenly Florabelle had an idea.
A great big rosy-red DREAMY idea.
    She wiggled her toes. Out popped
two bright petunia-pink fins. "I bet
the ocean isn't so scary . . . when
you're a *mermaid*!"
    She ran to the water's edge. And sure
enough, it was just as she'd imagined.

"Florabelle Jean, you're swimming!"
"We're so proud of you!"
"Let's play!" Florabelle giggled. "The water feels great!"

At home, Florabelle
brushed her teeth,

combed Marigold,

and climbed into her perfectly made bed.
No one even had to remind her.

"Sweet dreams!" she called from her pillow. "I love you!"

And as Florabelle dove into a sea of rosy-red dreams, her mother picked a strand of sea jewels from her hair. "We couldn't dream of loving you more."

(This time, Florabelle Jean heard every word.)